Tiana Mermaid

By Henry Davis

Illustrations by Deepali

PAGE PUBLISHING, INC.
New York, NY

First originally published by Page Publishing, Inc. 2018

ISBN 978-1-62838-056-9 (Paperback)
ISBN 978-1-62838-057-6 (Digital)

Printed in the United States of America

eep Within the "Boobiest Sea," lived a pretty little mermaid named, Tiana. The only creatures that lived in the "Boobiest Sea," were sea horses, sea turtles, Mermaids, whales, dolphins, sharks, and on the bottom of the sea were the skeletons.

The only thing that they feared was the Electric Sharks. The E-Sharks didn't bother anyone unless someone came within their territory in the sea.

Tiana Mermaid was a happy little mermaid, and wow, could she swim fast. Tiana could even swim faster than all of the sea horses. She also had the gift of miracle healing powers. If anyone got hurt or sick, all she had to do was touch them with her hands and they would begin to feel better. Creatures came from all over the "Boobiest Sea," just to see or be healed by the famous Tiana Mermaid. Tiana Mermaid, was famous through out the sea for her powers and her kindness. Everyone who knew her loved her.

One day Tiana Mermaid was swimming around chillaxing and enjoying the coolness of the water. While swimming along, she saw a sea turtle stuck between two sharp coral reefs. The sea turtle had gotten a deep gash in his shell from the coral reefs. When Tiana noticed it, she felt sorry for the sea turtle, and felt that she should help him.

"Hi, Mr. Sea Turtle. I'm Tiana Mermaid and I am going to help you. I can't free you but I'll get you some help."

"Oh, thank you, Ms. Tiana Mermaid."

"Just call me Tiana."

"Okay, I will and I have heard of you. You do wonderful things to help sick and wounded creatures of the sea. I have been stuck here for days and I feel very weak."

"Don't worry, once I call my friends to free you, I will take good care of you." said Tiana.

Tiana Mermaid used her telepathic powers to summon her sea horse friends. They came instantly to Tiana's call. Tiana showed them the problem and they knew just what needed to be done.

Once they freed the sea turtle, Tiana used her healing powers to heal Mr. Sea Turtle. All of a sudden, Tiana started to glow in the darkness of the sea. The water all around her lit up. Mr. Sea Turtle's eyes opened up wide as Tiana put her hands on his shell. The turtle started to shake and glow from her touch. Just like magic the gash in the turtle's shell began to close up. Once he was healed, Tiana removed her hands.

The sea turtle was so happy that he began to cheer, "It's a miracle! It's a miracle! Yay! Yay! Yay!" He swam around with a great big smile. "Thank you! Thank you, Tiana Mermaid. You my dear are truly a miracle! I am going to be your friend forever!"

"You are welcome, Mr. Sea Turtle. But what is your name?"

"My name is Silly. Silly sea turtle."

"What kind of name is that?"

"Well, I was given that name because I do silly things, like getting myself stuck between coral reefs. I would have never gotten out if you had not come along and saved me."

"Mr. Sea Turtle we have to change your name."

"What name do you have in mind, Tiana?"

"How about we call you Na-Na?"

"You've got to be kidding?"

"No, I am not kidding. I am very serious. Every time that you are about to do something silly, we will always say Na-Na to let you know that's not cool to do."

"Oh, you've got jokes, huh, Tiana?"

"Besides, it is the end of my name 'Tiana,' and I like that name for you because you are special to me."

"Ah well, since you put it that way, Na-Na it is." The sea horses all agreed that it was a cute and special name with a ring to it.

It was that time of the year, when the "Boobiest Sea" starts to prepare for Halloween.

A week before Halloween and Tiana and Na-Na didn't have a costume for the Biggest Halloween party in Boobiest sea history.

Na-Na wanted to go dress up as a whale but that wasn't original. Besides, Na-Na could not fit in a whale costume.

So Tiana said, "Hey, Na-Na. I know what would be perfect for us to wear to the party and I bet you that one of us is sure to win the contest for best costume."

"And what might that be, Tiana?" Na-Na said with a raised eyebrow.

"We can go as rappers!"

"Ah, ha ha, ha ha! Girl, you know you are funny, Tiana."

"What's so funny? You can go as Lil' Wayne with the dread locks and everything."

"Tiana, let me ask you something. Have you ever, ever, ever seen a turtle with dread locks, a mic, and a gold necklace filled with diamonds?"

"No?"

"Well, I guess you're in for a treat."

"And guess who I am going to be Na-Na?"

"Who?"

"I am going as Missy Elliot. No, on second thought I am going to as Ms. Janet Jackson. Janet, if you're sassy! We'll be the *bomb!*"

"Yeah, Tiana, you got that right! Mr. Bling Bling and Ms. Sing Sing! Check me out Tiana. Shake it fast, watch ya self, show me what ya working with."

"Na-Na, that's Mystical, not Lil' Wayne."

"Girl, don't hate, appreciate. I'm doing my thing. Anyway, who are the judges going to be, Tiana?"

"I asked the whales and the dolphins to be the judges. They said that they would be glad to do it."

"Okay, let's do it! You already know!" And the two friends sealed the deal with a high five.

There is another event at the Halloween party of the Boobiest Sea called the "Jack-O-Lantern Hunt." You have to swim all over the bottom of the sea and find the glowing pumpkin. Yes, it glows in the water, in the darkness of the watery sea, with its scary face.

Tiana Mermaid, swam all around the Boobiest sea, except where the E-sharks lived, to remind everybody of the upcoming Halloween party and to wear a costume. She told the skeletons at the bottom of the sea, and everybody else that she could remember. The skeleton bones were clicking and clacking with joy over the news. This was the only time of the year that the skeletons could actually have some fun.

"It's on! It's Halloween, October 31st and it's time to *parrrty!*" Said one of the skeletons.

The sea turtles and the sea horses brought food, games, and music. They even hooked up a new game, bobbing for apples.

Have you ever bobbed for apples under water? It's fun but don't drown.

Unknown to Tiana and her friends, the E-sharks were planning to crash the party. Their only costume were killer E-sharks, which is what they really were.

When the party started, it was poppin' and everybody was chillin' and having fun. Na-Na took off his shell and was dancing and doing his thing. He had everyone chanting, "Go Na-Na! Go Na-Na! Go Na-Na! Go! Go!"

Actually, Na-Na won the dance contest. Although he had great competition. He almost lost the contest when one of the skeletons showed up and did the Harlem Shake. His bones were clicking and clacking to the beat. But Na-Na held him off when he broke out and did the Superman. The judges went crazy and so did the crowd.

Tiana won the costume contest, of course, as Ms. Janet "Sassy" Jackson. When Na-Na, busted out looking like Lil' Wayne under water, he scared everybody so bad that they started hiding!

Tiana's telepathic powers told her that something was wrong. All of a sudden the killer E-sharks came out of nowhere and completely surrounded the party. There had to be at least a hundred of them. There was no escape. Although she was scared, Tiana approached the leader of the killer E-sharks.

"Please don't eat us, Mr. King E-shark." She said.

The King E-shark had a hungry look on his face. He looked at Tiana Mermaid with his angry face and said, "We weren't invited but we came to party. Is it okay?" The King E-Shark smiled.

"Sure, you guys can party with us. We didn't invite you because we were all afraid of you," said Tiana Mermaid.

"There is no reason to be afraid of us. We only eat people who try to capture or kill us. We are really nice, once you get to know us."

"Well let's party!" said Tiana, and everybody cheered. Then the party continued.

Tiana, was proud and happy to announce that the King E-shark was the winner of the Jack-O-lantern Hunt. From that day on, all of the creatures of the Boobiest Sea loved and cared for each other. They lived in perfect harmony.

THE END

Do You Remember…?

1. How many sea creatures are in the story? _____

    _____

2. Who won the dance contest? _____

    _____

3. What was Tiana doing when she was swimming in the coolness
   of the sea water? _____

    _____

4. If someone was hurt or sick, what did Tiana do? _____

    _____

5. Who are Mr. Bling Bling and Ms. Sing Sing? _____

    _____

Answers: 1. Eight. Mermaids, sea horses, sea turtles, whales, dolphins, skeletons,
e-sharks, and octopus. 2. Silly the sea turtle. 3. She was chillaxing. 4. She would use
her powers to help them. 5. Mr. Bling Bling is Silly, and Ms. Sing Sing is Tiana when
they are in their Halloween costumes.

Word Association
Match the words in Column A with their most likely partner in Column B

Column A:

Tiana ____

Corral ____

The Harlem ____

Electric ____

Sea ____

Silly the ____

Column B:

____ Sea Turtle

____ Sharks

____ Mermaid

____ Horses

____ Reef

____ Shake

About the Author

Henry Davis is a New York City based author and poet. Although born in Charleston, S.C., Davis was raised in the West Side of the Bronx as well as the Harlem sections of New York.

A retired Marine, Davis found the transition back into civilian life difficult. Coming from this difficult background, Davis managed to turn his life around, riding a wave of positivity, and creating a life that would bring respect to him and to those around him.

Davis is a caring person who believes that children of all ages should be exposed to positive messages. He uses his vivid imagination, his gift with words, and his humor to deliver inspiring and educational lessons to children.

When not creating stories for children everywhere, Davis is a carpenter and an electrician. He spends his free time with his daughter, Tiana, who he cites as his greatest creative inspiration.